ANT SANG
SHAOLIN BURNING

HarperCollins*Publishers*

FOR DELIA, HENRIETTA, AND FREDERICA.
MY FAMILY, MY CENTRELINE.

WRITTEN WITH THE ASSISTANCE OF A GRANT FROM

ARTS COUNCIL OF NEW ZEALAND TOI AOTEAROA

HARPERCOLLINSPUBLISHERS
FIRST PUBLISHED IN 2011
BY HARPERCOLLINSPUBLISHERS (NEW ZEALAND) LIMITED
PO BOX 1, SHORTLAND STREET, AUCKLAND 1140

HARPERCOLLINSPUBLISHERS
31 VIEW ROAD, GLENFIELD, AUCKLAND 0627, NEW ZEALAND
25 RYDE ROAD, PYMBLE, SYDNEY, NSW 2073, AUSTRALIA
A 53, SECTOR 57, NOIDA, UP, INDIA
77-85 FULHAM PALACE ROAD, LONDON W6 8JB, UNITED KINGDOM
2 BLOOR STREET EAST, 20TH FLOOR, TORONTO, ONTARIO M4W 1A8, CANADA
10 EAST 53RD STREET, NEW YORK, NY 10022, USA

NATIONAL LIBRARY OF NEW ZEALAND CATALOGUING-IN-PUBLICATION DATA

SANG, ANTHONY, 1970-
SHAOLIN BURNING / ANT SANG.
ISBN 978-1-86950-813-5
1. CHINA-HISTORY-QING DYNASTY, 1644-1912-FICTION.
I. TITLE.
741.5993-DC 22

ISBN: 978 1 86950 813 5

COVER DESIGN BY SIMON RATTRAY
INTERNAL DESIGN BY ANT SANG

PRINTED BY GRIFFIN PRESS, AUSTRALIA, ON 100GSM WOODFREE

1
THE TALE BEGINS

JOURNEY TO THE CAVE OF LONG SLEEP

AS I APPROACH THE CAVE, I RECALL WHAT MY *SIFU** OFTEN *TOLD* ME.

'WHEN I TEACH YOU *KUNG FU*, I'M *NOT* TEACHING YOU HOW TO *FIGHT* ...'

*TEACHER

'... I'M TEACHING YOU HOW TO *LIVE*.'

5

MAGNIFICENT ESCAPE OF THE FIVE ELDERS

IT STARTED YEARS AGO

AT THE *SHAOLIN TEMPLE* ...

FROM WHAT I'VE HEARD, THEY DIDN'T SEE IT COMING ...

... IT SEEMS *INCREDIBLE* THAT THE MONK ON WATCH THAT NIGHT

DIDN'T NOTICE *THREE HUNDRED* OR MORE MANCHU *SOLDIERS*

AMBUSHING THE
SHAOLIN TEMPLE.

THEY DIDN'T STAND A CHANCE THAT NIGHT.

NO ONE SHOULD HAVE MADE IT OUT *ALIVE* ...

AIM!

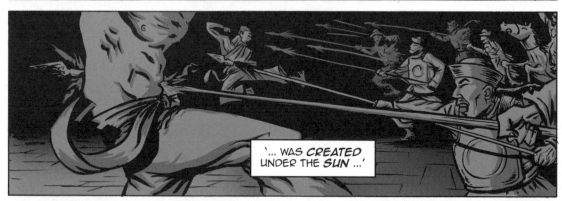

... *LEGEND* SAYS *FIVE* MONKS ESCAPED THE *INFERNO* THAT NIGHT ...

... 'THE FIVE ELDERS'.

BUT THOSE WHO WERE *THERE* KNOW DIFFERENTLY.

THERE WAS *ANOTHER*.

A *SIXTH* ...

... AND HE WOULD SET *CHINA* ON *FIRE*.

2
THE ADVENTURES OF DEADLY PLUM BLOSSOM

FORTUITOUS RESCUE AT SONGSHAN BABY TOWER

OH ...

SPLISH

SPLISH

DON'T THINK I *WANTED* THIS ...

PLEASE. I DIDN'T COME TO FIGHT.

PUZZLING RETURN OF THE KILLER TONGS

YUNNAN ...

... SOUTHERN CHINA.

FIFTEEN YEARS LATER ...

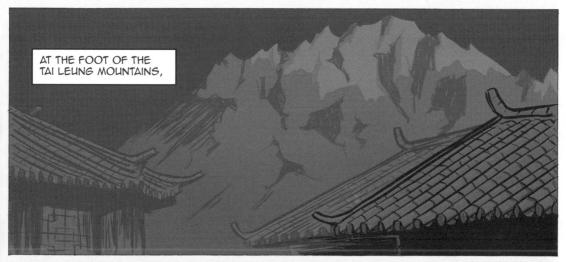

AT THE FOOT OF THE TAI LEUNG MOUNTAINS,

WHILE THE WHOLE VILLAGE SLEEPS,

THIS IS WHERE WE PRACTISE OUR ART.

... C'MON, *HURRY UP!* I DON'T WANT TO *MISS A THING* ...

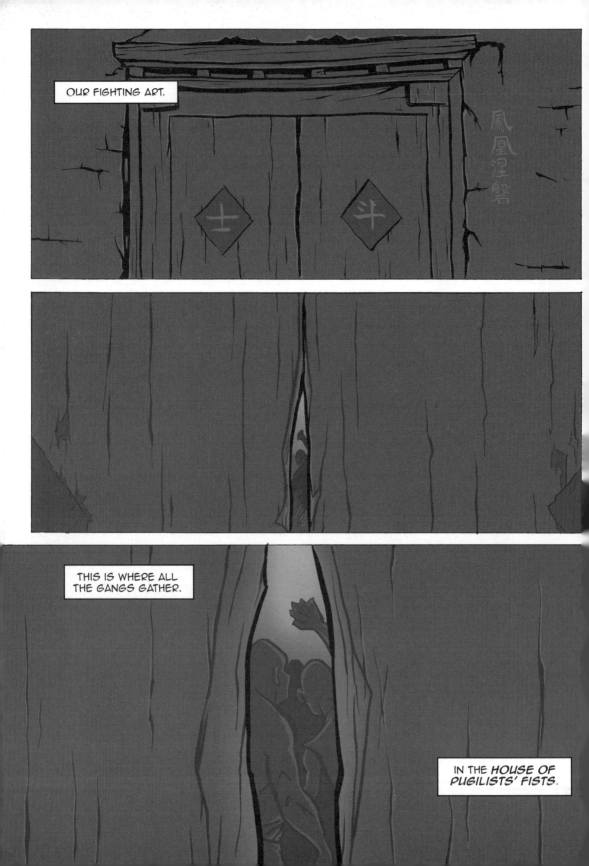

OUR FIGHTING ART.

THIS IS WHERE ALL THE GANGS GATHER.

IN THE *HOUSE OF PUGILISTS' FISTS*.

THE MALEVOLENT
FISTS OF SUICIDE.

THE DRUNKEN GLORY
OF BARLEY WINE GANG.

THE BENEVOLENT LAUGHING MONKEY PALM GANG.

THE LYRICAL AND GENTLE SUPPLE FEET OF TRIUMPH,

THIS IS *ILLEGAL*, OF COURSE ...

... THE *MANCHU* HAVE FORBIDDEN OUR *SUBVERSIVE ART*.

THEY KNOW OUR MARTIAL ARTS ARE A *THREAT* TO THEM.

BUT HERE IN THE *DEEP SOUTH*

WE ARE, FOR NOW, *SAFE* FROM THE REACH OF THEIR SOLDIERS ...

39

41

... WHAT *RUMOURS?*

THEY SAY HE'S *GIVEN UP.* AND THE REST OF YOU ... YOU'LL *NEVER* AMOUNT TO *NOTHING!*

WELL, LET'S *SEE* ABOUT THAT. IF YOU WANNA FIGHT, *FIGHT ME!*

WELL?

THIS IS *BULLSHIT!* SIX DAYS FOR *THIS!*

KICK HER *ARSE,* BRO ...

I THINK ONLY *NOW* AM I BEGINNING TO UNDERSTAND WHY THEY CAME BACK THAT LAST TIME ...

BECAUSE THE *HOUSE OF PUGILISTS' FISTS* IS LIKE *NO OTHER* PLACE IN THIS LAND.

WITHIN THESE FOUR WALLS, WITH OUR *HANDS* AND *FEET*

WE CREATE *ART.*

WE EXPRESS OURSELVES

IN WAYS WHICH ONLY WE CAN UNDERSTAND.

AND FOR A MOMENT WE ARE *FREE.*

THE KILLER TONGS WERE *SEARCHING* FOR SOMETHING THEY HAD *LOST* A LONG, LONG TIME AGO ...

NO.

THEY HADN'T RETURNED FOR *ADMIRATION* OR *PRAISE* ...

THEY WERE SEARCHING FOR THE *FIRE*.

AND AS THEY DISAPPEARED INTO THE DARKNESS THAT NIGHT,

DRAWN FORWARD ON THEIR JOURNEY TOWARDS *FAME* AND *IMMORTALITY* ...

... NOBODY IMAGINED THAT WOULD BE THE *LAST* WE WOULD *EVER* SEE OF THEM.

UNVERSED DISCIPLE OF THE WHITE CRANE TEMPLE

THE MOST **IMPORTANT** PRINCIPLE TO REMEMBER IS TO **PROTECT YOUR CENTRELINE.**

THIS **PROTECTS** YOUR EYES, NECK AND ALL YOUR **VITAL ORGANS** ... IT FORCES YOUR OPPONENT TO ATTACK IN A **CIRCULAR PATH**, WHICH IS AN INDIRECT PATH, AND THEREFORE SLOWER ...

... **CONTROL** THE **CENTRELINE** AND YOU **CONTROL THE FIGHT.**

NOT ONLY DO YOU USE THE CENTRELINE FOR **DEFENCE**, USE IT ALSO FOR **ATTACK.**

MY **PUNCH** IS **UNORTHODOX.** IT IS DECEPTIVELY **SHORT** AND **DIRECT**, BUT WHEN PERFORMED CORRECTLY HAS **DEVASTATING POWER.**

... SHE HAS A CRUCIAL FIGHT SOON, BUT HAS *NEVER* FOUGHT BEFORE. SHE HAS BEEN GRANTED *ONE YEAR* TO PREPARE.

HI ...

I SAW YOU FIGHT THE *KILLER TONGS* LAST NIGHT. YOU WERE *AMAZING* ...

UH HUH.

I'VE BEEN A FAN OF YOURS FOR *AGES* ... I WISH I HAD EVEN *HALF* YOUR SKILLS!

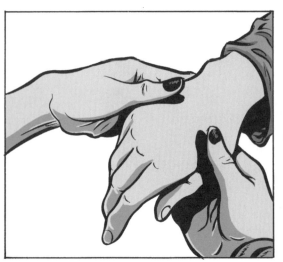

YOU CAN'T BE SERIOUS ... SHE'S GOT HANDS LIKE A *BABY'S BUM*. SHE WON'T BE READY IN A YEAR!

SHE *WILL* FIGHT IN A YEAR WHETHER SHE'S *READY* OR *NOT*. THERE IS NO CHOICE IN THE MATTER. I WILL PREPARE HER AS BEST I CAN IN THAT TIME ... I THOUGHT YOU'D FEEL *LIKEWISE!*

OK ... I'LL HELP WHEN I *RETURN* ... I PROMISE!

THE LEGEND OF MA TI FU KEN

HE WAS *DIFFERENT* FROM THE REST OF US.

HE DIDN'T *WALK* ...

HE *RAN*.

AND WHILE WE ALL *LOVED* TO FIGHT,

HE *LIVED* TO FIGHT.

MARTIAL ARTS WERE AS *NATURAL* TO HIM

AS *BREATHING*.

THERE WERE *RUMOURS* ABOUT HIM ...

'HE TRAINS *ALL NIGHT.*'

'HE DOESN'T SLEEP.'

ONE NIGHT A *STORM* RIPPED THE GIANT *LYCHEE TREE* FROM THE *GROUND.*

BUT SOME SAY IT WAS *MA TI FU KEN* ...

... AND THAT HE *FELLED* IT WITH A *SINGLE PUNCH.*

STILL OTHERS CLAIM HE *SCALED* THE *TAI LEUNG MOUNTAINS* ...

... *WITHOUT* STOPPING EVEN *ONCE* TO CATCH HIS *BREATH.*

BUT THERE WAS *ONE* THING ALL OF THE GANGS COULD *AGREE* ON ...

... *MA TI FU KEN* WAS THE *GREATEST FIGHTER* IN THE WHOLE OF *YUNNAN PROVINCE.*

BAR *NONE.*

... AND YET HE HAD HIS SIGHTS SET ON *GREATER THINGS* ...

HE DREAMT OF LEAVING HIS MARK ON THE *WHOLE* OF *CHINA.*

AND WHO BETTER TO TEACH HIM THAN THE *MURDEROUS MONK* WHO FOR *FIFTEEN YEARS* HAD *TERRORISED* THE *COUNTRY.*

SOME SAY HE *RAN* ALL THE WAY AND *DIDN'T STOP* UNTIL HE *FOUND* HIM.

BUT NO MATTER HOW *FAR* OR *FAST* HE *RAN* ...

HE COULD *NEVER* OUTRUN THE *FIRE.*

THE PERILOUS JOURNEY TO DUNTOW

68

70

CACK!

FFFFIIIIIPPPP

CONVERSATION AT YUNNAN TEAHOUSE

EVEN THOUGH WE HADN'T *SEEN* HIM FOR *MONTHS*,

MA TI FU KEN'S DEATH LEFT A GAPING *HOLE* IN OUR *WORLD*.

HE HAD LEFT THE SAFETY OF YUNNAN TO *MASTER* THE *ART* OF *FIGHTING* ...

... AND DIED IN *PURSUIT* OF *GREATNESS*.

SO I WONDER, IF *EVEN HE* COULDN'T MAKE IT ...

... WHAT DOES THAT *MEAN* FOR THE *REST* OF US?

ANOTHER *BARLEY WINE*, PLEASE ...

YOU *COMMISERATING* TOO, EH?

YEAH, I CAN'T BELIEVE *HE'S GONE*.

ALL *THREE* OF THEM, *GONE!* JUST LIKE THAT!

'*THREE* OF THEM'? *WHO* ARE *YOU* TALKING ABOUT?

THE *KILLER TONGS*, OF COURSE! KILLED BY THAT *MURDEROUS MONK*. POOR BASTARDS.

THEY WERE *YUNNAN'S FINEST* PUGILISTS!

THE *KILLER TONGS*?! BUT THEY WERE JUST *HERE* THE OTHER *WEEK* ...

YEAH. *BLOSSOM* FOUGHT THEM!

THEY *WEREN'T* SO GREAT. I HAD THE BETTER OF 'EM. OUR MATE *MA TI FU KEN*, HE WAS YUNNAN'S *BEST*!

MA TI FU KEN? IF HE'S SO GREAT, WHY HAVEN'T *I* HEARD OF *HIM*?!

THE KILLER TONGS MADE A *LIVING* FROM THEIR TALENTS. THEY PUT THEMSELVES TO *GOOD USE*. YOU *RABBLE* SHOULD *LEARN* FROM *THEM*. MAYBE THEN WE WOULD TAKE YOU *SERIOUSLY* ...

MA TI FU KEN WAS *GONE*.

AND TO *HONOUR* HIM, WE MUST *DEDICATE* OURSELVES TO THIS *FIGHTING ART*.

NO MORE *GAMES*. IT'S *LIFE* OR *DEATH* ...

... WE MUST PROVE OURSELVES. WE MUST DO SOMETHING TRULY *MAGNIFICENT*.

THE FATEFUL DECISION OF DEADLY PLUM BLOSSOM

84

OUR STYLE IS *REVOLUTIONARY*. IT WILL BE CHAMPIONED BY *WOMEN* FOR ALL TIME ... AND SO WILL *YOU* IF I NAME OUR STYLE AFTER YOU – '*PLUM BLOSSOM FIST*' KUNG FU.

YOU DON'T UNDERSTAND, I *HAVE* TO DO THIS ...

I SAY I WILL CONSIDER HER *GENEROUS OFFER* DURING THE NIGHT.

BUT SHE *KNOWS* ME *BETTER* THAN THAT.

THERE'S *NO DECISION* TO BE MADE ...

SIFU SAYS YOU'RE A *WILD* ONE ...

... WELL, THIS IS MY *FIRST* SOLO RIDE ... SO YOU BE *GOOD* FOR ME, Y'HEAR?

NNNGH.*

*PISS OFF!

LIKE A *LYCHEE TREE* SPROUTS *FRUIT,*

SO I'M A *FIGHTER* ...

IT'S WHAT I *DO.*

I SHOULD HAVE BEEN *DEAD, UNWANTED* AND *FORGOTTEN* AT THE *BOTTOM* OF A *BABY TOWER*, ALL THOSE YEARS AGO.

I DECIDED AT AN EARLY AGE, I WOULD *NEVER* BE SO EASILY *FORGOTTEN*.

AND THAT *SINGULAR* PURPOSE HAS *SUSTAINED* ME EVER SINCE ...

... TO PROVE I'M *WORTHY* OF THIS *LIFE*.

STEADY, BOY ...

NUNNGH!*

*SHIT!

3
THE STORY OF MONK WHO DOUBTS

A BUDDHIST PARABLE

OH?

THANK YOU, MONK!

THE TORTUROUS ORIGINS OF HE WHO HAS TURNED HIS BACK ON ALL WHICH IS BRIGHT AND WONDROUS

I'M HERE TO LEARN *KUNG FU.*

NOT OLD *SUPERSTITIONS*

NOR SPIRITUAL *NONSENSE ...*

MONK!

WAKE UP!

YOU'RE HAVING A *BAD DREAM ...*

MONK ...

HUH?

SSSH!

I SHOULDN'T BE HERE ... I *MUST* GO.

HE'S *WATCHING* US ...

BAH – THE *BUDDHA* IS A *FOOL!*

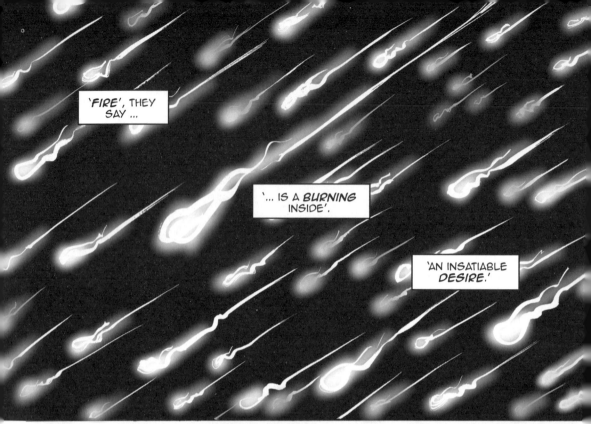

'FIRE', THEY SAY ...

'... IS A BURNING INSIDE'.

'AN INSATIABLE DESIRE.'

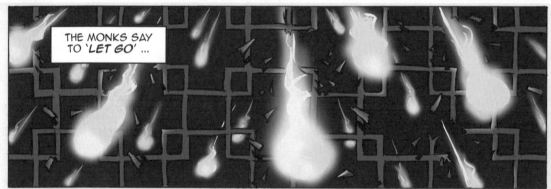

THE MONKS SAY TO 'LET GO' ...

... BUT WHAT DO THEY KNOW?

'IF YOU CANNOT **CONTROL** THE **FIRE** ...'

'... IT WILL **CONTROL YOU.**'

'USE YOUR TALENTS *WISELY* ...'

'... OR YOUR *TALENTS* ...'

FFSSSSSSSSSS

SSSSS-TUK!

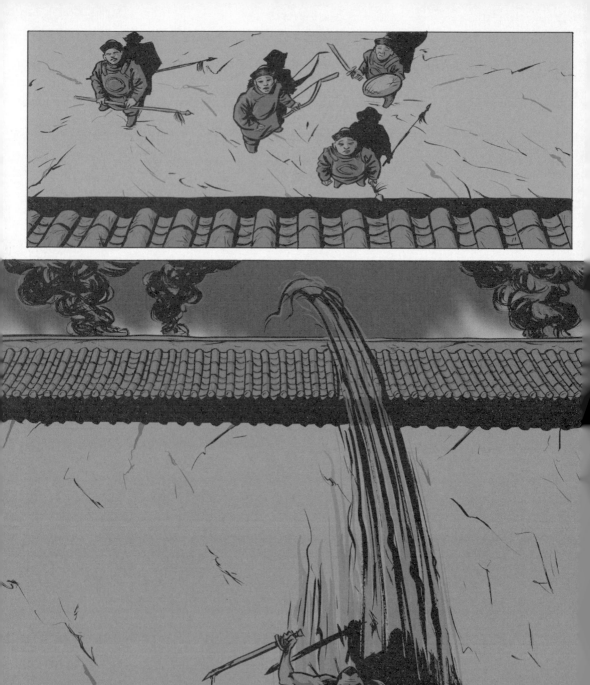

KK-CHUNI

WHAT *USE* ARE YOUR *MARTIAL ARTS* ...

... IF YOU *REFUSE* TO *USE* THEM?

...

ABBESS NG MUI, STEP ASIDE ...

RIIIPP!

BROTHER ... *CLOTHE* YOURSELF. *SHARE* MY ROBE ...

... THE STREETS WILL BE AWASH WITH MANCHU BLOOD!
MARK MY WORDS, EVERY LAST ONE RESPONSIBLE FOR THIS WILL DIE!
THIS NIGHT I ABANDON MY LIFE AS A MONK ...
... I VOW TO UNLEASH A FIERY HELL ACROSS ALL OF CHINA FOR WHAT HAS HAPPENED TONIGHT.
AND FROM THIS MOMENT ON ...
... I SHALL BE KNOWN BY THE NAME 'HE WHO HAS TURNED HIS BACK ON ALL WHICH IS BRIGHT AND WONDROUS'.

THE TERRIBLE SHADOW OF VENGEANCE

FOR FIFTEEN YEARS I'VE WALKED THIS LAND ...

... LIKE A GHOST NOW.

I'M BARELY HUMAN ANY MORE.

THEY ALL KNOW WHY
I'M HERE ...

... AND THAT THEIR
TIME IS SURELY UP.

AND THOUGH IT WAS
ONCE JUST SOLDIERS
I DESPATCHED,

BEFORE LONG IT WAS
THEIR WIVES ...

... MOTHERS

AND CHILDREN.

BEFORE LONG ...

COUNTERSTRIKE OF THE SHUNZI EMPEROR

SLAM!

A *TRAP?*

WE WILL LURE HIM IN AND FROM THERE WE SHALL *CUT HIM DOWN.* WE MUST MAKE A *PUBLIC DISPLAY* OF HIM ...

... 'BY KILLING *ONE* WE WILL *WARN ONE HUNDRED.'* THE PEOPLE WILL SOON LEARN WHO CONTROLS THIS COUNTRY WHEN THE DREADED MONK IS KILLED BY *DEATH OF A THOUSAND CUTS.*

AND TO MAKE ALL THIS HAPPEN, I HAVE REQUESTED THE SERVICES OF SOME *SPECIAL MEN.*

LET ME *INTRODUCE* YOUR IMPERIAL MAJESTY TO ...

I HAVEN'T YOUR **APPETITE** FOR **VIOLENCE** ...

... WITH ALL DUE RESPECT, UNLESS WE MAKE A **CRUEL EXAMPLE** OF THIS **BASTARD**, YOUR IMPERIAL MAJESTY WILL **NOT** EARN THE **RESPECT** OF THE POPULATION.

LEAVE IT TO **ME**, AND I WILL PROVE **VIOLENCE** IS THE **GREATEST ASSET** TO YOUR IMPERIAL MAJESTY'S **DYNASTY**.

AMBUSH AT INSPIRING SUCCESS TOWER

WHY AM I DOING THIS?

WITHOUT *PURPOSE* ...

... THIS IS ALL *MEANINGLESS*.

I CAN *NEVER* BRING HER BACK.

THERE'S NO PURPOSE HERE ...

... OTHER THAN *EGO.*

THE MONKS TRIED TO *WARN* ME ...

... 'LET GO.'

'LET GO OF EVERYTHING ...'

'... AND WHAT REMAINS ...'

'... IS WHAT IS TRULY YOURS.'

AND IN THE BACK OF MY MIND, I KNOW THEY WERE *RIGHT* ...

... BUT IT'S TOO *LATE* NOW.

SLAM!

WELCOME!

YOU HAVE PROVED ELUSIVE FOR TOO LONG ...

... I'M PLEASED TO FINALLY *MEET* YOU!

CLANK

LET US *CELEBRATE,* EH!

IT'S PATHETIC.

HE'S A *HIRED* KILLER.

A HACK.

HE *THINKS* HE'S ON *FIRE* ...

... BUT HE'S SO *NOT* ON *FIRE*.

CLANK

CLANK
CLANK

... AN *INFERNO*.

SHIT!

HE'S
COMIN'!

RARGHH!

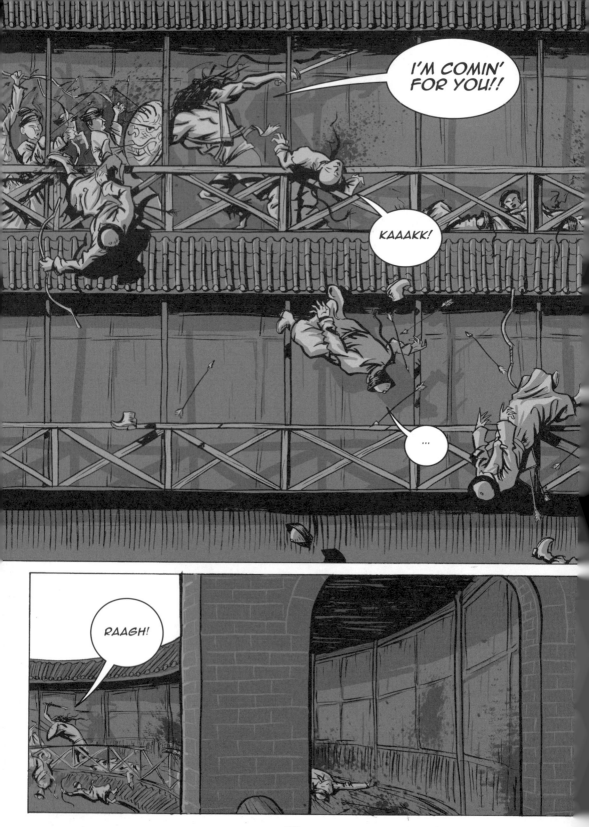

PLEASE! YOUR FIGHT IS WITH ME! PLEASE DON'T TOUCH HER!

... OF ALL MY CONCUBINES, SHE IS MY ONLY LOVE. IF YOU HAVE ANY COMPASSION, PLEASE PROMISE ME SHE WILL BE SAFE.

YOU *LOVE* THIS WOMAN?

...

I VOWED TO *KILL* EVERY LAST ONE OF YOU *MANCHU* UNTIL I HAD YOUR *HEAD* IN MY *HANDS*. BUT SEEING YOUR DEVOTION FOR THIS WOMAN, I'VE CHANGED MY MIND ...

DONGGO!!!

NOW WE'RE *EVEN* ... I'M *FINISHED* WITH THIS *WRETCHED GAME.*

NO, THERE'S NO *PURPOSE* TO THIS ANY MORE.

LITTLE JADE, IF YOU COULD SEE WHAT HAS *BECOME* OF *ME*, YOU WOULD BE TRULY *ASHAMED* OF WHAT I HAVE ACHIEVED.

THE *FIRE* HAS *GONE OUT*, AND FOR MY ACTIONS, I WILL *BURN* IN AVICI NARAKA* FOR THE LONGEST OF TIME.

*BUDDHIST FIERY REALM OF HELL

YOU ...

... ARCHER, ARE YOU *ALIVE?*

THERE'S A BANNER OF *CAVALRYMEN* IN THE *NEXT VILLAGE.* TELL THEM WHAT'S HAPPENED ... *TRACK* THAT *BASTARD!* BRING ME HIS *HEAD!*

THE INFAMOUS BATTLE OF ONE THOUSAND DEATHS

I WANT NO PART OF THIS.

IF YOU **MUST** COME, THEN COME. AND I WILL HAND YOU YOUR **DEATH** ...

... BUT YOU SHOULD *TURN AROUND.*

GO HOME TO YOUR *COMFORTABLE* LITTLE LIVES ...

... TO YOUR *WIVES,* YOUR *CHILDREN.*

GO *CARE* FOR YOUR *ELDERS.*

SLEEP PEACEFULLY AT NIGHT.

YOU'VE **NO** BUSINESS HERE.

THIS IS A PLACE FOR THE **CURSED**.

THERE'S **NOTHING** HERE.

YAAARGH! YARRRGH!!

NOTHING BUT ...

MISERY.

... I CAN'T *LET GO.*

4
DEADLY PLUM BLOSSOM
VS
MONK WHO DOUBTS

... WELL, I WANT TO *SEE* IF THAT'S *TRUE!*

I SPENT *MONTHS* IN THE *DESERT* TO FIND YOU ...

GO HOME, LITTLE GIRL. YOU'VE NO BUSINESS HERE ...

I CAME A *LONG* WAY FOR THIS *FIGHT* ... I'M *NOT* LEAVING 'TIL I GET IT.

DRIFTED *IN* AND *OUT* OF CONSCIOUSNESS

FOR WHAT SEEMED LIKE *MONTHS*

CHK

CHK

CHK

CHK

TO A MONOTONOUS *THUMP, THUMP, THUMP* AND FALLING *RUBBLE.*

AT TIMES I'D AWAKE TO FIND HIM *HOVERING* ABOVE ME ...

... *WATCHING* ME INTENTLY.

OR TENDING MY FEVER

WITH *UNEXPECTED* KINDNESS.

CHK

CHK

... SO THE *MAN* I CAME TO *KILL* WAS *NURSING* ME BACK TO *HEALTH.*

... *THANK YOU* FOR RETURNING ...

I DIDN'T UNDERSTAND ...

IN THE DARKNESS OF THE CAVE

I LOSE TRACK OF DAYS AND NIGHTS.

I'M TRAPPED HERE ...

... HELPLESS.

AND AMIDST THE *DARKNESS* AND *DELIRIUM*

A THOUGHT CREEPS UP ON ME ...

AND TAKES *HOLD*.

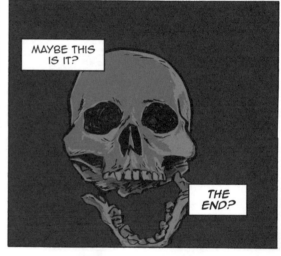

MAYBE THIS IS IT?

THE END?

FOR A MOMENT I *YEARN* TO SEE *HER* AGAIN ...

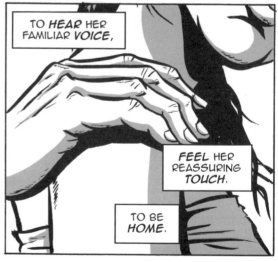

TO *HEAR* HER FAMILIAR *VOICE*,

FEEL HER REASSURING *TOUCH*.

TO BE *HOME*.

... AND IT DAWNS ON ME

THAT IF I *DIE* IN THIS CAVE ALONE,

WHETHER I WAS THE BEST PUGILIST IN *YUNNAN*

OR THE *WHOLE* OF *CHINA,*

IT *HARDLY* SEEMS TO *MATTER.*

AND I BEGIN TO *UNDERSTAND* WHAT SIFU MEANT

WHEN SHE SAID ...

'WHEN I *TEACH* YOU *KUNG FU* ...'

'I'M *NOT* *TEACHING* YOU HOW TO *FIGHT,*'

'I'M *TEACHING* YOU HOW TO *LIVE.*'

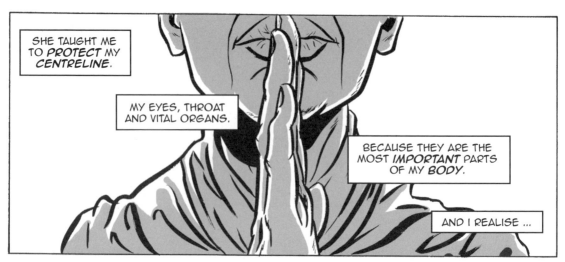

SHE TAUGHT ME TO *PROTECT* MY *CENTRELINE*.

MY EYES, THROAT AND VITAL ORGANS.

BECAUSE THEY ARE THE MOST *IMPORTANT* PARTS OF MY *BODY*.

AND I REALISE ...

OR *NOTORIETY*.

THE MOST *IMPORTANT* PART OF MY *LIFE* IS NOT *FAME*.

IT'S THE PEOPLE I *LOVE*.

THEY ARE MY *CENTRELINE*.

THEY ARE WHAT I MUST *PROTECT*.

AND I DECIDE ...

I *MUST* RETURN *HOME.*

WATER?

TELL ME ... I CAME HERE TO *KILL* YOU ... WHY ARE YOU *SAVING* ME?

YOU DIDN'T COME TO *KILL* ME ...

... YOU CAME TO *SAVE* ME.

186

... AND, AT LAST, *GOODBYE*.

THIS GIRL WHO CAME TO RESCUE ME ...

... I DIDN'T EVEN KNOW HER NAME.

I TELL HER, WHEN WE RETURN HOME, I WILL TRAIN HER FOR HER BIG FIGHT ...

... AND THAT WE WILL *NAME* OUR *KUNG FU STYLE* IN *HER* NAME.

SHE *LAUGHS*.

'IT'S NOT VERY FEROCIOUS,' SHE SAYS.
SO I TELL HER ...
... 'KUNG FU,'
'IT'S NOT ABOUT FIGHTING ...'
'... IT'S ABOUT LIFE.'
ANT SANG 2010

PAGE 7: THERE ARE MANY CONFLICTING VERSIONS OF THE DESTRUCTION OF THE SHAOLIN TEMPLE. THE DATES OF THE DESTRUCTION ARE COMMONLY ARGUED TO BE 1641 (BY ANTI-MING REBELS), 1647 (UNDER THE SHUNZI EMPEROR), 1674 (UNDER THE KANGXI EMPEROR) OR 1732 (UNDER THE YONGZHENG EMPEROR). THERE IS ALSO DISAGREEMENT AS TO WHICH OF THE TEMPLES WERE DESTROYED, AS THERE WAS A NORTHERN TEMPLE IN HENAN PROVINCE AND A SOUTHERN TEMPLE IN FUJIAN PROVINCE.

PAGE 12: TIGERMEN WERE A DIVISION OF THE MANCHU BANNER FORCES USED LARGELY FOR BREAKING UP THE ENEMY'S CAVALRY CHARGES. THEIR FEROCIOUS COSTUMES AND LOUD SHOUTING WERE MEANT FOR SCARING THE ENEMY, AS WAS THEIR USE OF FIRECRACKERS ON THE BATTLEFIELD.

PAGE 16: WHILE THE ESCAPE OF "THE FIVE ELDERS" IS WIDELY CONSIDERED TO BE MYTH, MANY KUNG FU STYLES TRACE THEIR LINEAGE TO ONE OF THE FIVE ELDERS.

PAGE 18: BABY TOWERS WERE USED FOR DISPOSING OF UNWANTED BABY GIRLS. THEY WERE ALSO USED BY THOSE PARENTS UNABLE TO AFFORD A PROPER BURIAL FOR THEIR DEAD BABIES.

PAGE 20: FEMALE INFANTICIDE IN CHINA DATES BACK TO AT LEAST 250 BC. DROWNING WAS THE MOST COMMON METHOD OF INFANTICIDE, THOUGH SUFFOCATION AND ABANDONMENT WERE ALSO COMMON.

PAGE 52: NG MUI IS SAID TO HAVE DEVELOPED WING CHUN KUNG FU AFTER SEEING A FIGHT BETWEEN A STORK AND A SNAKE. SHE SYSTEMATICALLY DESIGNED WING CHUN KUNG FU AS A STYLE WHICH COULD BE TAUGHT MORE QUICKLY THAN TRADITIONAL SHAOLIN KUNG FU BUT WAS BASED ON THE MOST EFFECTIVE ASPECTS OF THE TRADITIONAL STYLES.

PAGE 57: YIM WING CHUN IS SAID TO HAVE BEEN LIVING WITH HER FATHER IN YUNNAN, WHERE THEY MADE A LIVING SELLING TOFU AND FOODSTUFFS AT THE MARKET. WHEN A LOCAL THUG TRIED TO FORCE HER HAND IN MARRIAGE, NG MUI OFFERED TO TEACH HER KUNG FU TO PROTECT HERSELF AND BEAT THE THUG IN A CHALLENGE MATCH.

PAGE 62: MA TI FU KEN IS A FICTITIOUS CHARACTER BASED ON NEW ZEALAND CARTOONIST MARTIN 'FUCKEN' EMOND. MARTY WAS AN INSPIRATION TO MANY LOCAL CARTOONISTS AND TRAGICALLY DIED IN 2004. PAGES 62-64 ARE A HOMAGE TO MARTY AND ARE BASED ON SOME OF HIS UNPUBLISHED WORK.

PAGE 125: THE SHUNZI EMPEROR ASCENDED TO THE THRONE OF THE QING DYNASTY IN 1644, AT THE AGE OF FIVE. EARLY IN HIS REIGN, POWER WAS ACTUALLY HELD BY APPOINTED REGENTS. HIS REIGN AS EMPEROR WAS SHORT-LIVED AND ENDED WHEN HE WAS JUST 23 YEARS OLD, UNDER MYSTERIOUS CIRCUMSTANCES.

PAGE 127: GENERAL WU SANGUI WAS A COMMANDER OF THE MING ARMY. HE OPENED THE GATES OF THE GREAT WALL AT SHANGHAI PASS IN 1644, ALLOWING THE MANCHU ARMY TO INVADE CHINA FROM THE NORTH. HE LATER DEFECTED TO THE QING DYNASTY, PURSUING AND EXECUTING THE WOULD-BE MING EMPEROR IN YUNNAN IN 1661.

PAGE 152: IT IS SAID THAT DONGGO, SHUNZI'S FAVOURITE CONCUBINE, DIED OF HEARTACHE AFTER THE DEATH OF HER BABY IN 1661. COMMON BELIEF IS THAT SHUNZI CONTRACTED SMALLPOX SHORTLY AFTERWARDS AND DIED ALSO. A LESS COMMON BELIEF IS THAT SHUNZI DID NOT DIE, BUT ABANDONED THE LIFE OF AN EMPEROR AND BECAME A MONK.

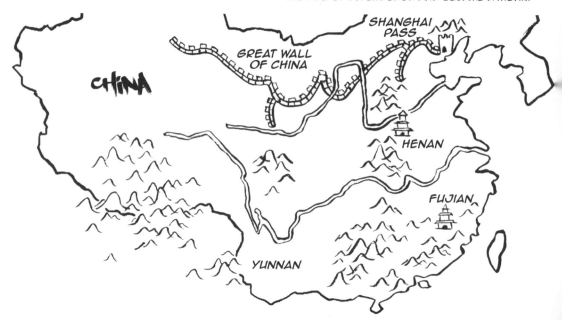